12/09

fresh fruit pie - yum!

carving pumpkins

No Eat Not Food

The search for intelligent food on planet earth

664-A Freeman Lane, PMB 888
Grass Valley, CA 95949-9630
(888) 224-9997
www.MountainPathPress.com
Email: Info@MountainPathPress.com

Also by Rick Sanger & Carol Russell:
"Are There BEARS Here?"
"Do Teddy Bears Ski?"

Special thanks to all those who helped me so much in growing this book. Eileen Schell, Jim Cahill, Rachael Mazur, Eric Engles, Clara Bergamini (age 12), Kiran Ferrini (age 9), Sage Mann (age 10) and many others, gave me wonderful suggestions for the text; Dianna Winslow for remaining steadfast in her support of all my crazy projects; Blossom Sanger (Mom!) supplied inspirational artwork (see her beautiful floral images at www.FloralPortraits.com); Claire Wasserman (age 16) and Yarra Pasner (age 10) gave me precise and candid feedback; George Sanger (Dad!) for proofing the text; and the Brownlie household for my wonderful compost birthday cake.

The font used in this book, Carol 2, was derived from the handwriting of Carol Russell. The text is printed on 50% recycled paper (post-consumer waste) that is certified by the Forest Stewardship Council whose intent is to eliminate habitat destruction, water pollution, displacement of indigenous peoples and violence against people and wildlife that often accompanies logging (http://www.fscus.org).

Publisher's Cataloging-In-Publication Data
(Prepared by The Donohue Group, Inc.)

Sanger, Rick.
  No eat not food : the search for intelligent food on planet earth / [by Rick Sanger ; illustrated by Carol Russell].

  p. : ill. ; cm.

  ISBN: 978-0-9653149-2-3

1. Food habits--Juvenile literature. 2. Sustainable agriculture--Juvenile literature. 3. Organic farming--Juvenile literature. 4. Natural foods--Juvenile literature. 5. Nutrition--Juvenile literature. I. Russell, Carol. II. Title.

TX355 .S2285 2006
641.1   2006926874

For Mom:
Wild, wise, woman. Thank you for feeding my body,
my mind, my soul. -RS

For Mom and Dad:
Who gently seeded my imagination in our
backyard organic garden. -CR

A very special thanks to Michelle Vesser. Her guidance over 15 years has led me gently toward a deeper understanding and appreciation of nourishment, and has given me insight into the political, spiritual, agricultural and social forces that influence it. And to all the other farmers like her: guardians of our precious agricultural knowledge and wisdom.
Agriculture is humankind's first and most important technology.

Chapter One

At first, it didn't seem like the day was going to be different from any other day. Our backyard looked the same as it always did. Our bushes were their usual bushiness, the trees their usual treeziness, and Ralph, our dog, was itching his usual itch. But the deafening *Whoosh... Boom* wasn't normal, the flying dirt wasn't normal, and the thing that looked like a VW bus that plummeted from the sky and demolished our swing set was *definitely* not normal!

Jen came running out of the back door, shouting "What did you do now?!" She thinks that just because I'm her little brother that everything's my fault.

"Shhhh! Over here!" I motioned to her and we both peered around the corner of the house.

"What is it?" Jen asked.

"It looks like a '67," I replied, poking my elbow into her ribs.

"Stop goofing around! It's obviously some sort of alien spacecraft," she whispered, "And something's moving..." As we watched, the driver's door flopped open.

"Yikes..." Jen muttered, "look at *that!* I hope it doesn't have a ray gun!"

Ralph's tail curled down and he started to whimper a little.

The Thing looked around slowly until it faced us.

"TAKE!" it squeaked.

"I think it's trying to speak..." Jen said.

"ME!" it squawked.

I could only gawk.

"TO YOUR..." then it paused.

"...leader?" I asked.

"FEEDER!" it answered. "Take me to your FEEDER!"

Jen whimpered, "It's hungry! It's gonna eat us!"

Ralph began to back away.

"Jen! Give it one of your chips!"

Jen remembered the nacho-flavored snacks clutched in her hand. "Studies show," I advised her under my breath, "that 9 out of 10 aliens prefer Macho Nacho Crispies over human flesh."

She took out a chip and threw it toward the Thing, but the air caught it and the chip just fluttered to the ground at our feet. "Run for it!" Jen shouted as she took off away from me.

My heart leapt, my mind leapt, but my legs were stuck in the thick goo of fear! The Thing started toward me. Closer and closer it came... I closed my eyes as it slowly reached out – but then I peeked. Whew! It had picked up the chip.

"Food?" it asked me in a creaky-door voice.

"Food!" I happily assured it.

Its antennas gingerly touched the chip and flinched away.

Finally, it proclaimed with disgust:
"Not Food!"

It flicked the chip over its shoulder,
"No Eat Not Food!"

The Thing looked down at Ralph and Ralph started barking. "Food?" it asked me.

"No!" I exclaimed. "Ralph! Ahh... dog! Not Food."

Ralph ran to his food bowl. The Thing walked to the bowl, examined it carefully with his antennas and once more proclaimed, "Not Food. No Eat Not Food."

"It must be a picky eater," I said. "Even I've eaten dog food."

"What *is* food?" Jen asked.

"We better figure it out," I said, "before we start looking like life-sized candy bars."

"That's it!" she said. Jen ran into the house and quickly returned with a candy bar. It must have come from her secret stash, the one I'd been looking for since Halloween.

But the Thing was now wandering down our street. It had a little jump to its walk: Step, step, hop! Step, step, hop!

"Hey. Where's it going?" Jen asked.

"I'll bet it's off to forage in the neighborhood," I said. "If we're lucky, it'll like the taste of Old Man Crodgers!"

"Don't you wish!" Jen said and ran down the street after it. "Hey! You! Mr. Thing! Candy! Food!"

I jogged along to keep up, hopping every third step like it did. "Hey!" I shouted, "Dude! We've got food!"

It must have heard us, because it turned its head around. But its body kept moving forward. That looked weird.

It pointed its antennas at the candy bar and after only a moment, it again announced, "No Eat Not Food!"

Jen stopped running and put her hands on her hips. I could tell she was getting frustrated. "OK, Mr. NoEat," she said, "suit yourself. Find your own food!"

"I think that's what he's doing, Jen. Look, he's heading right for the supermarket. Let's go see what happens!"

Jen shrugged her shoulders, "Sure. Why not?"

NoEat was in the third aisle by the time we caught up with him. That's the aisle with all my favorite cookies. His antennas were spinning around like crazy, but he didn't slow down or pick anything up.

Up and down the aisles we went. "Excuse me..." I asked a grocer whose head was hidden deep in one of the lower shelves, "which aisle has alien food?"

Jen yanked my arm, "Will you *pleeease* act sane," she pleaded, "just this once?!"

"Sure!" I said. I put my hands over my head and waved them around like antennas, saying, "No Eat Not Food! No Eat Not Food!"

When we rounded the next aisle, we nearly ran right into NoEat. He had stopped in the vegetable section; his antennas were perfectly still.

"Jen, is that noise coming from him?"

"Yeah," she said, "I think his stomach's growling."

"Food?" he asked.

"Sure!" I said, "Food!"

He carefully lifted a tomato off the top of the pile and took a bite. He smacked his jaws a little – then turned and spat out the sticker.

"Not Food," Jen and I said at the same time as No Eat.

The vegetable man came over and peered through squinted eyes at NoEat's face. He wasn't sure what he was seeing.

"This is our friend, NoEat," Jen explained, "He's... ah... not from around here."

"Oh," said the grocer, "I see... Does he like the tomatoes?"

"Food," NoEat said, carefully tasting the pulp of the tomato, "...and Not Food!" He suddenly seemed distressed. "Food plus Not Food! Food Plus Not Food! Must find F.F.F! Must stop F.F.F!"

"What the heck does *that* mean?" I whispered to Jen.

"Where food from?" NoEat asked us.

"Right here!" I told him. "All our food comes from this supermarket."

"Food not grow here! Food not born here! Where food from?" NoEat squawked again.

"From the warehouse," the grocer said. "It all comes from the warehouse!"

"Where how? What where how?"

"No," the grocer explained, "the **ware**house. Trucks bring everything here from a big building where it's been stored."

NoEat pulled out a shiny object from his belt. It looked like a small, silver staircase with a knob on the back - like a tiny doorknob. When he twisted the knob, something strange happened. He disappeared! But it wasn't like he suddenly *popped* and was gone. It was more like he climbed up an invisible staircase. It's hard to describe. It's even harder to tell you why I followed him. I ran to the place he had disappeared and could feel the invisible steps with my feet. I felt for one, then the next, and began to climb up after him.

Chapter Two

"We probably shouldn't be doing this!" Jen warned from behind me. But climbing up invisible stairs is something everyone should try. The first few steps may make you feel dizzy, but it gets better once your head passes through the ceiling and pops through the floor in a new place. When it happened this first time, I found myself in the back of a large truck filled with crates of tomatoes.

Jen bumped into me. "Quick!" she said, "There he goes!"

I saw NoEat's legs disappear on the stairs above me, so I scrambled up after him. Next, my head popped through the pavement outside a huge building. There were five or six trucks backed up to the building and fork lifts were bringing out crates of tomatoes and loading them into the trucks.

NoEat was close by, looking around. "Food not from here! Nothing born here!" he was saying.

"This crate says 'D & G Mega Farms,'" Jen said. "Maybe the tomatoes are from there."

"Food from farms?" NoEat said, thinking this over. Then suddenly he announced, "F.F.F. farm!" and once again climbed up the stairs out of sight.

We rushed to follow him. After a few hazy steps, my vision cleared and I found myself standing in dirt. We were in a field that stretched out as far as I could see. Row after row of tomato plants extended all the way to the horizon. Big machines were grumbling nearby. It was kind of spooky.

Jen whispered from behind me, "There he is!" I turned around and saw her pointing at NoEat. "And there's his ray gun. I *knew* it!"

We crouched down; his back was toward us. "Why does he have his ray gun out?" I asked. "Is he gonna shoot the tractor?"

"...or us!" Jen whispered. "I'd better..." she suddenly jumped up and ran at NoEat.

NoEat turned and the beam from the gun swept around. I dove to the ground. With the dirt so close, I could see a bunch of dead bugs right in front of my nose. Did the ray gun do that?

"It's OK!" Jen called to me. When I looked up, she was brushing herself off. NoEat was lying on his back, unconscious.

"Whoa! What did you do?" I asked.

"Nothing! He was looking at something in the bushes, started wobbling, then just fainted." Jen walked over to NoEat and took his ray gun.

"Can you wake him up?" I asked, "Try giving him mouth-to-mouth resuscitation."

"Don't be gross. Besides, that doesn't work on aliens," Jen said, "...at least I don't think it does..."

"It doesn't," a new voice said, "I've tried it."

We looked up and saw a girl's head floating in the air.

"Who are *you*?" I asked.

"LuLu's the name. Farming's the game."

"LuLu," I said, "hate to be the one to break the news, but your body's missing."

"Really?" She looked down, "Oh, I see," she said, and stepped out into view. "It's an alien transporter. Kinda feels like riding an elevator."

"An elevator?" I asked her, "and here we've been stuck using the stairs."

"Look, that's a friend of mine," LuLu said. "Will you help me get him back to my place?"

There were fuzzy little hairs on No Eat's arms and legs that kind of tickled, but he didn't weigh much. We carried him into the invisible elevator, then everything went black.

Chapter Three

When the elevator doors opened, we were in a strange, alien world. Instead of row after row of tomatoes, we were surrounded by flowers and vegetables of all kinds and colors. I noticed the sound of birds right away. LuLu went over to a nearby bush, picked a strange yellow fruit, then squeezed its juice into NoEat's mouth.

"What is *that*?" Jen asked.

"It's a tomato. He loves tomatoes," LuLu said.

"It sure doesn't look like any tomato *I've* ever seen," Jen commented.

"Me neither!" I added. "What kind of weird planet is this?"

LuLu smiled and thought for a second.
"This is planet LuLu," she declared, "...and
I am the queen!"

NoEat mumbled. "Food..." he said, "Food...
Yum LuLu Tomato!"

"Note to self," I thought, "Aliens prefer mouth-
to-tomato resuscitation."

NoEat and LuLu hugged and talked excitedly
in some high-pitched, squeaky language
until NoEat pointed at us.

"He wants you to try some of my
tomatoes," LuLu said.

"You first," Jen dared me. It
was always like that with
Jen, which is how she
got me to taste
dog food.

The smell of the tomato was luscious, like a thousand sweet tomatoes all contained in this one. The taste was even better... it was sweet and tart; like summer heat and a cool river. I wiped its juice off my chin. The tomato was tons more tasty than any I had ever had, yet somehow I knew it was what tomatoes were *supposed* to taste like. "Wow!" I said, then quickly added, "Jen, you won't like it. Better give me yours."

I had used that trick on Jen before; it just wasn't gonna work this time. She bit into her tomato immediately and, from the look in her eyes, I could tell she liked it as much as I did.

In a deep, kinda fake voice, LuLu said, "This is only a small fraction of the delights we can offer you earthlings. You need only join us in overcoming the F.F.F."

With my mouth full of tomato, I asked, "Wha fa ef ef ef?"

"It's an invisible force that controls your mind and limits your view of the future," LuLu explained. "Under its influence, people poison the air, pollute the water, and grow lifeless food. Unchecked, it can starve an entire planet! But with your help, we can stop the spread of the F.F.F."

"Was that what NoEat was doing with this ray gun?" Jen asked.

NoEat and LuLu looked at each other. "Sure!" she said suddenly, "Do you know how to use it?"

"Not really," Jen said.

LuLu pointed, "See that chili pepper bush? Let's pretend it is a short-sighted zombie possessed by the F.F.F. Just aim and pull the trigger."

NoEat was watching all this and chirped a little when Jen lifted the ray gun. He looked at LuLu and LuLu looked back at him. He chirped again but then held his breath.

"Do It!" LuLu commanded.

Jen pulled the trigger, but instead of bursting into flames, the bush lit up in a strange glow, threw back its branches and said, "Hola Senorita! ¿Te puedo ayudar?"

Jen's eyes got big and her knees grew weak; she lowered the beam. The plant stopped glowing, but a big fat worm popped up where the beam was now pointing and said "Hiya Jen! Beautiful day, don't ya think?"

Chapter Four

LuLu burst into laughter when the worm talked. NoEat was chirping like crazy, so he must have thought it was funny, too. But Jen just stood there, still in shock. NoEat picked another yellow tomato and offered it to Jen.

"Did that plant... talk?" Jen asked.

"Don't worry," LuLu said, "You see that's not a ray gun, it's a translator beam. It lets NoEat talk to other forms of life here on earth. By the way, it's good you call him NoEat since his real name sounds like a herd of hyper hamsters."

"Wait a minute..." Jen said, "We're on earth? You told us we were on an alien planet."

"No, I was just kidding. This is good ol' earth. NoEat and his family landed on our farm a long time ago. They're the ones who taught me about the F.F.F. and how the translator beam is better than any weapon to counter it."

"There's that F.F.F. again," Jen said, "What *is* the F.F.F. anyway?"

"It's a *fooorce,*" I said with my fingers sticking out like claws, "it takes over your *braaaiin!*"

LuLu giggled. "He's kinda right! The F.F.F. stands for 'Forces of False Food.' It's easy to understand: If a chair won't hold a person, then it isn't a real chair. If a house doesn't keep the rain out, it isn't a real house. And if food isn't healthy, it isn't real food — so we call it False Food."

"Oh. You mean junk food," I said.

"Not just junk food," LuLu replied. "Let's say growing a tomato causes pollution. Everyone knows that pollution hurts the environment and a dirty environment hurts humans. Since there's pollution from growing that tomato, then the tomato isn't healthy. Not healthy: Not food."

"Growing tomatoes causes pollution?" I asked.

"It depends on how it's done," LuLu answered. "For thousands of years, humans grew food organically — that is, their methods didn't harm the environment. But then people started to use new methods — methods that pollute. They started using artificial fertilizers, which wash off fields into nearby streams. They started using pesticide poisons to kill insects and herbicide poisons to kill weeds."

"All those poisons..." Jen said, "Why?"

"At first it seemed to help plants grow. People didn't want to know that all those poisons were slowly damaging the soil and polluting the environment. That's exactly how the F.F.F. works — it hides the future. People get excited about having something they want and forget to think hard about how that thing might affect the future. It's easy to be controlled by the Forces of False Food."

"What does false food look like?" Jen asked.

"Sometimes it hard to recognize," LuLu said. "That's why I carry these..." She pulled out two rulers and held one up to a tomato. As she did, the tomato seemed to grow larger and larger, as if the ruler was a magnifying glass. "That checks out," she said.

She put the first ruler away and held up the second. Once again, the tomato seemed to grow large when viewed alongside it.

"What are those?" I asked.

"Rulers!" LuLu said, as if it were obvious. "This one measures how healthy the food is, and this one measures whether its been grown in a sustainable way."

"What does sustainable mean?" I asked.

"It means you can keep doing it forever and ever," LuLu explained. "Let's say year after year you use poisons to help grow your plants. Someday, there will be too much poison around and *nothing* will grow. So using poisons isn't sustainable. Or what if you use too much water - then you might wash away all the top soil or run out of water. That's not sustainable either."

LuLu pulled out a shiny object. It looked like a small, silver elevator with a knob sticking out the back - like a tiny doorknob. "Come with me and I'll show you how these rulers work." She twisted the tiny knob and stepped into that strange elevator. We followed her and once again, everything went black.

Before I knew it, we were all on that dusty tomato farm once again. There was a bitter smell in the air. LuLu whispered to us, "Here we are at a farm caught in the grip of the Forces of False Food. But how do we know this? Everything looks normal... or does it?"

She held the "Sustainable" ruler up to one of the tomato plants. It seemed to get smaller and smaller, like we were looking at it through the wrong end of a telescope. "You see?" LuLu said, "This farm is growing false food. And I bet I know why." LuLu held the ruler up to a small tube at the base of the plant.

"What is that?" I asked.

"A feeding tube," LuLu explained. "The soil here is so sick, the tomatoes can't live here on their own. They have to be fed dinosaurs."

"You're crazy," I said. "Dinosaurs can't fit through those tubes."

"Course not," she said. "It's fertilizer that comes out of these tubes. But the fertilizer is made from natural gas. Natural gas is like oil; it's made from dinosaurs and other critters that died millions of years ago."

"Wait a minute," Jen said, "Isn't the oil supposed to be running out? Our mom keeps telling us we need to conserve gasoline because the oil is running out."

"Exactly!" LuLu said, "And so is natural gas. *That's* why using dinosaurs for fertilizer isn't sustainable."

Then, LuLu pulled back a branch; we could all see the dead bugs that had been hidden behind it. NoEat turned green... I mean... more green than he usually was. He squeaked quietly and said, "Food plus Not Food."

"Guess I don't need to pull out my other ruler," LuLu said. "This isn't a healthy place."

The sound of a nearby tractor caught our attention. Like wings extending from its body, two long pipes were spraying a mist over the plants to either side of it. LuLu took the translator beam from Jen. She turned it on and pointed it toward the tractor.

"What are you spraying?" LuLu said into the translator. The farmer on the tractor straightened up as if awakening from a cloudy dream. Although he didn't turn toward us, we knew he could hear what LuLu was asking.

"Pesticide." We could hear the farmer's thoughts coming out of the translator.

"What's it for?" LuLu asked.

"Kills bugs. They've been eating my tomatoes."

"Isn't spraying poison on food a bad idea?" LuLu asked, "Won't it hurt whatever eats it?"

"We wash 'em off before we sell them... and I need to sell them to support my family. Come on, all my neighbors do it. Even my father used pesticides."

"But not now?" LuLu asked.

"My father passed a few years ago, after a sickness..."

"Oh. I'm sorry," LuLu said.

"It's just been on my mind lately," admitted the farmer.

"You know," LuLu said into the beam, "I was sick once. For two months I didn't have the strength to get out of bed. My parents were very scared. My father paced back and forth each night. He was a farmer too; he used pesticides and fertilizers too. But his crops were sick and now his daughter was sick. He began to wonder if both were caused by the same thing. Do you think that's possible?"

"I don't know," the farmer thought, "Sometimes I wonder. The birds don't seem to be around as much. And there's no more fish in my stream. Only green slime. Each year I have to use more fertilizer to keep the plants healthy and more pesticide to keep the bugs away. I don't like it, but I've got to provide for my family. They're the most important thing in my life."

LuLu said, "My father finally decided there might be a chance that his poisons had caused my sickness. He decided to stop using them and he risked everything to do it."

"You got better, didn't you?" the farmer asked.

"I did. But now my mother is sick."

"Oh. That's no good," said the farmer.

"It scares me and it's sad," LuLu said, "but you know, she's your mother, too."

I turned to Jen, "Wait a minute..." I whispered, "how could they both have the same mother?"

After a few moments, the farmer's thoughts came through the beam. "The birds... the fish. I think I see what you mean."

"Then you understand," LuLu said, "that the earth is mother to us all. Without her we have no food or shelter. She holds us up our entire lives and embraces us when we die. If she is sick, then our human family is in trouble." LuLu thought for a moment, then said, "I have a gift for you. These belonged to my father and helped guide him through his changes. I hope they help guide you as well." She held the rulers in the beam. They floated over to the tractor seat next to the farmer where he'd find them.

LuLu turned the beam off. The farmer looked around like he wasn't sure who he'd been talking to. We all ran as fast as we could back to the invisible elevator and in a flash, we were once again in the sweet-smelling embrace of LuLu's farm.

The Last Chapter of the Book

"I need one of my universally famous carrots after that little adventure," LuLu said. She walked to a particular clump of green stalks, gave them a tug, and out of the ground popped some real-live carrots! "Vitamin A and beta carotene, anyone?" she asked. We took them, washed them with a hose, and gratefully munched away.

"Were you really sick?" I asked LuLu.

"I sure was," LuLu said. "It was quite a few years ago. Luckily, it was about that time that NoEat's parents landed in our field. With the help of the translator beam, we all became fast friends, nearly family! NoEat's parents taught us about the F.F.F. and the problems it created on their planet."

"What about those rulers? Where'd they come from?" Jen asked.

"My dad came up with the ruler idea," LuLu said, "and NoEat's dad figured out how to make them. But don't worry, he made plenty!" She reached in her bag and pulled out a whole handful of rulers. We all laughed. "You see, my mom liked to give them away. She realized that if us kids were going to have a healthy planet to live on, then a lot more people need to measure what they do against these rulers."

"I'd like to talk with more farmers about the F.F.F.," I said.

"You've talked with them quite a bit already," LuLu replied.

"What do you mean?" I asked.

"I mean, you've already been talking to farmers and bankers and grocers and senators, too. You've been telling all of them that growing false food is what you want."

"That can't be!" I protested, "I don't even know any farmers! My mind isn't possessed by any strange force!"

"Are you sure?" LuLu asked.

LuLu made me less sure than I thought I was.

"Every time you buy food, you talk to farmers," LuLu explained. "Your money tells the entire world what you want. And every time you buy false food, your message is clear."

I recognized the truth in what she said. If I only bought non-polluting tomatoes, then the farmer we met would still be able to support his family without having to use poisons.

NoEat's stomach gurgled. He squeaked, "LuLu famous carrot!"

LuLu pulled up another carrot, gave it to NoEat, took a big bite of her own and looked up at the sky.

"Food is so much more than just... food," LuLu said wistfully. "It's a whole experience! Take carrots: They remind me of the state fair. The pop of a good bite sounds like a dart hitting a balloon. And isn't the taste of it like being handed a big stuffed prize? But red peppers..." She picked a pepper off a nearby bush, "are less predictable than carrots. You never know whether to expect a tangy taste or a sweet taste or both at the same time. It's like hide and seek when you're just about to be found."

"What about peaches?" I asked.

"Peaches? You tell me," LuLu said. She picked one from the tree above us and gave it to me.

I closed my eyes as my teeth pierced through the tart outer skin. The sweet juice rolled down my chin. "Sweet and tart... sweet and tart... in circles..." I said. "It's a Ferris Wheel – on a warm night."

"And Jen, what do you think of these strawberries?" LuLu asked.

Jen took one. "They're small," she said.

"Don't underestimate small," LuLu warned her. "You would insult everyone here! Besides, looks can be deceiving; that's another trick used by the F.F.F."

"Right," Jen said. She put the strawberry into her mouth. After a while she opened her eyes. "It's my heart," she said, "I feel like I've gotten a wet kiss from a warm puppy."

"What about those plants over there?" I asked.

"Those are marigolds," LuLu said.

"You eat marigolds?"

"Sometimes!" LuLu giggled. "But those are to keep hornworms off our tomatoes. You see, everything here is a tiny piece of a huge puzzle, a puzzle that forms a picture of life and health and sustainability – a picture in which humans are just one piece. I don't understand how all the pieces fit together, I doubt anyone ever will, but I *do* know that the more pieces there are, the healthier my farm will be. And it's so beautiful! And so interesting! The longer I look at it, the more I see and learn. Last year I noticed a bat swooping around, eating mosquitoes, so I put a wooden box way up on that pole. A whole family of bats moved in and now they're eating thousands of mosquitoes every night – and their poop is great for the soil, too!"

"LuLu," Jen asked, "how can we tell farmers that we want them to grow real food like you do?"

"Just buy real food," LuLu said.

"But how do we know it's real food?"

"Ask. Ask if the food is organic. Ask if it's grown without oil-based chemicals. Go to a health food store and talk with the grocer, or just ask the farmer."

Jen was confused, "But I don't know any farmers."

"You know me!" LuLu said, "And I'm gonna make you part of my food club! I call it 'LuLu's Organic CSA.' Club members get lots of great food every week! Real Food. Organic Food. Food that's healthy for you now and healthy for the future, too. CSA clubs are a tasty way we can help each other to stay free from the Forces of False Food."

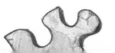

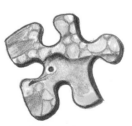

LuLu stopped walking. "Here we are! The compost pile! Hand me that translator beam, you've gotta see this." There were several mounds in front of us; one had layers of old plants, another was chocolaty brown and had a rich, earthy smell. It didn't look like much, but LuLu obviously loved it. She turned on the translator beam and pointed it toward the compost. In its light I could see worms, centipedes, and a thousand other tiny critters. I could hear a crowd of voices all singing and talking and telling jokes.

"Howdy all you critters!" LuLu called.

"Hi there, LuLu!" came a chorus of tiny voices. "Hey LuLu! We just made up a new cheer! Wanna hear it?"

"Sure!" LuLu agreed.

The bugs all let out a big cheer and shouted...

"What improves your mood?
FOOD!
Lick your chops and chew!
FOOD!
Improve your health!
It's nature's wealth!

Yeaaaaa...FOOD!

I watched as a pill bug was thrown into the air and caught by a jolly, fat grub.

"That is cool!" I said.

"I didn't know bugs could be so happy," Jen observed.

"Won't see *that* using pesticides," LuLu said, "These critters have plenty to eat, so our plants will have plenty to eat, so *we'll* have plenty to eat. What could be better?"

"Compost is plant food?" I asked.

"The best kind. Plants love this stuff. And it's free! All ya need is a zillion little bugs and fungi and bacteria... and *they're* free, too!"

LuLu held up her rulers. The compost was clearly healthy *and* sustainable.

NoEat started squeaking and squawking. LuLu listened for a while, then gave him a big hug. She announced, "NoEat has come here to tell me that he's going to travel and teach others how to grow food sustainably. He wants to fix his VW spaceship so he can be on his way."

NoEat turned and started walk-hopping away.

"Isn't he going to use his transporter?" I asked.

"Why would he? Your house is only a few blocks from here!" LuLu said. "If you look around, you'll find organic farms are
    closer than you think."

We followed along behind NoEat. "Is he going back to his home planet?" Jen wanted to know.

"That's no longer possible," LuLu explained, "You see, at one time huge farms covered his planet. They mostly grew Prickly Portino, a very important food for them. But the Portino Blight swept through the farms and killed all the Portino plants."

"A blight?" Jen asked.

"It's a disease that kills only one kind of plant," LuLu said, "so if you depend completely on that plant for food, then blights are bad news. That's why a healthy puzzle of life needs so many pieces — it needs diversity. Some on NoEat's planet saw what was happening and argued for change. But there was too much arguing and not enough listening. In the end, their planet was ruined. That's why NoEat's parents had to leave, and why NoEat can't go back."

"Why doesn't he stay at our school and teach about health and sutainability?"

LuLu looked at NoEat and NoEat looked at us. He let out some squeaky noises and gestured with his two top legs. "He believes you two can do that," LuLu explained. "Then he can go help others."

I thought about that. If I learned more from LuLu, or from my own small garden, then my friends could learn from me. In a sense, I'd be a piece of the puzzle, too. It wasn't a bad idea... it might even work!

Before I knew it, we had arrived back at NoEat's spaceship in our backyard. LuLu and NoEat worked on the engine, and I asked them every question I could think of about how to grow a garden. Finally, LuLu announced, "All fixed! Just hand us the gas." NoEat was looking at me and pointing.

I turned around, saw a can of gasoline, and handed it to them.

"No, No. Not that gas! Look in the box!" LuLu said.

I looked in the box that LuLu had brought from her farm and found a bag of organic pinto beans. "You mean, these?"

"That's it! The spaceship only eats Real Food, too!"

LuLu gave NoEat the big box of fresh vegetables from her CSA food club and he put it into his spaceship before climbing in. I raised my arms over my head like antennas and waved. "No Eat Not Food!" I shouted. NoEat waved and shouted back, "No Eat Not Food!" He put the spaceship in gear and zoomed away.

Later that evening, I was getting ready for bed. I was going to start my own garden in the morning and was wondering if Prickly Portinos would grow on Earth. How could I call NoEat and ask him? Maybe LuLu would know. I pulled open my dresser drawer to get my pajamas. What I saw there took my breath away.

On top of my clothes were two green rulers and what looked like a small, silver phone with a knob sticking out the back...

The Compost Times

All the News That's Fit to Compost   Vol 1 Num 1

The Inside Scoop on LuLu's Organic Farm
Secrets Revealed

Reporter: LuLu, is it true you have aliens living on your farm?

LuLu: I have no comment at this time.

Reporter: If you aren't in contact with aliens, then where did you get those yellow tomatoes?

LuLu: I grew them myself! Tomatoes come in all kinds of colors: yellow, orange, green, white, striped... even black. I grow twelve types here and I chose those from a catalog of over 500 different types.

Reporter: Be real. I've only seen one kind of tomato and it's red. Where are the others?

LuLu: You've only seen the common, red tomatoes that are cheap to grow on large, industrial farms. Look around. You'll find blue potatoes and purple string beans. Carrots come in white, purple, black, red, green and yellow. Once you start looking, you can find over 100 different kinds of lettuces and over 5000 varieties of potatoes! I like choosing my vegetables based on their taste, not on whether they are cheap to farm with a machine. When profit comes before taste, you can suspect the F.F.F. is at work. If you'd rather pick *your* vegetables based on taste, go to a farmer's market, a health food store, join a CSA or just grow your own!

Reporter: What does CSA mean, anyway?

LuLu: The letters stand for "Community Supported Agriculture." A CSA club is when people like you pay a farmer in advance to grow healthy food for you. Usually, you'll get a new box of vegetables every week. You pay for it all in advance so the farmer has the money to do his or her job. CSAs are good for you, farmers *and* the planet. One of my favorite farms is the Full Belly Farm in California. If you go to their website, www.FullBellyFarms.com, you can see what their CSA members got in their boxes this week.

Reporter: If I joined your CSA, would I get organic food?

LuLu: Of course!

Reporter: And organic means it's grown without pesticides?

LuLu: That, and a lot more. The idea behind organic farming is to raise food in the healthiest possible way for people *and* the planet. The most obvious thing is not to use poisons anywhere on the farm. But also, organic

farmers don't use chemical fertilizers or sewage sludge; they don't grow bioengineered plants; and they don't sterilize with radiation. They try to conserve soil and water for the benefit of future generations.

Reporter: Is that why organic food is more expensive?

LuLu: Organic food *isn't* more expensive. Often you'll pay less money for non-organic food, but that's because it's stolen.

Reporter: Stolen? From where?

LuLu: From the future. Growing non-organic food steals the health out of the soil, the air and the water. Someday,

somewhere, someone is going to need to clean up that mess in order to grow more food. It's going to be very expensive; *that's* the cost that is missing from the price tag of non-organic food. Growing non-organic food is stealing from people of the future who will be trying to grow food for themselves.

Reporter: If chemical fertilizer is supposed to feed plants, why is it bad to use?

LuLu: Like I told Ricky...

Reporter: Who is Ricky?

LuLu: You know, Jen's brother.

Anyway, like I told Ricky, the supply of chemical fertilizers isn't endless. That's because these fertilizers are made with ammonia, ammonia is made from natural gas, and natural gas, like oil, comes from buried dinosaurs. I think it's interesting that natural gas is not only an ingredient of ammonia, but is also used to fuel the high temperatures needed to *make* ammonia. Even *more* oil-based products are used to package those fertilizers, deliver them, and drive the tractors that spray them! So if you grow your own tomatoes using compost, you'll be saving gas, too!

Reporter: Oh. So fertilizer isn't really bad for the environment, it's just not renewable.

LuLu: Hold on there! That's just part of the story! You see, plants use less than half of the fertilizer that is put in the fields. The rest seeps into the ground where it pollutes water supplies, or evaporates into the air and becomes acid rain. Most often, it flows off the farm into streams. But algae, a tiny plant that lives in water, loves to eat it! The algae grows out of control, sucking all the oxygen out of the water. Without oxygen, most other critters can't live. The natural ecology in the water is ruined.

Reporter: Wait a minute, I think I've seen a pond covered in slimy, green mats near D&G Mega Farms on the other side of town. Is that algae?

LuLu: Sure is. I know the pond you are talking about. NoEat and I were just there and he could taste the pesticides.

Reporter: Who is NoEat?

LuLu: He's... uh... not from around here.

Reporter: Oh, I see. What pesticides did he taste?

LuLu: He drew me their chemical diagrams. One of them has bromine in it and is called methyl bromide. It is a very dangerous chemical if you are a bug, a weed, a nematode,

or a human. Another is called chloropicrin and a third is called 1,3-dichloropropene. All these, and many more, are legal to use on non-organic farms.

Reporter: But they wash off, right? Just like the farmer said. Right?

LuLu: The United States Department of Agriculture tests foods for the presence of pesticides. It's called the Pesticide Data Program. The foods are washed and prepared just like you would do. But pesticides are still found. Some pesticides are purposely made so that they're hard to wash off. That way they'll stay on plants in a rain storm. Other pesticides are taken up into the plant, and end up inside the part you eat.

Reporter: Is there any way for me to tell if a tomato or apple or orange has pesticides on it?

LuLu: Nope.

Reporter: What about some sign, like those warning labels on cigarettes.

LuLu: The only sign is the "certified organic" label. But you'll only find that on food *without* poisons on them.

Reporter: Isn't that backwards? Shouldn't we be told when something is dangerous instead of when something is safe?

LuLu: Hmmm... that's a good point. Sounds like you need to talk with your congressman about the F.F.F!

Reporter: I'll do that. Oh yeah, while I'm thinking of it, I remember seeing green tomatoes out on D&G Mega Farm, so I guess I *have* seen tomatoes that aren't red.

LuLu: You saw unripe tomatoes. Unripe tomatoes are always green. When industrial farms grow tomatoes, they never let them ripen. They pick them when they are still green and tough so that they can be shipped in trucks without damage. Once they arrive at their destination, they are exposed to ethylene gas. That

Local Author Eats Compost

Rick Sanger, local author, was recently given a birthday cake made to look like compost. *"It's delicious!"* he said, but insisted that the best part was that few of his friends wanted to even try the cake. *"I had it mostly to myself."*

Artist Transformed by Work

After finishing work on the book <u>No Eat Not Food,</u> artist Carol Russell says, *"It's important work - it changed me in a way that's difficult to describe. Even my friends have noticed that I'm different now."* Russell encourages everyone to read the book, adding, *"it may transform the world in ways we can't even imagine."*

makes them turn red so people *think* they're ripe. But the only way for the taste to reach its full flavor is if the tomato stays on the plant, being fed all the way until its perfect, ripened state.

Reporter: But if the plant has to feed the tomato until it's ripe, then what feeds the plant?

LuLu: The plant has to get everything it needs from the air and soil that surround it. Remember, it can't walk down the street to buy a snack, so the farmer has to make sure it has

what it needs. My plants seem to like compost the best.

Reporter: What exactly is compost?

LuLu: It's plants and vegetables that have been eaten by fungi, insects and bacteria.

Reporter: You mean just decaying vegetables?

LuLu: Yep! And everything decays, so compost is pretty easy to make! Just make a pile of garden clippings and kitchen waste in the corner of your yard and it will eventually become compost. There are some tricks to make the pile decompose more quickly, such as making sure it stays damp and mixing it every so often so it gets lots of oxygen.

Reporter: Some of our readers don't have a very big yard. Can they still make compost?

LuLu: Oh yes! I think the most fun way is to make a red worm farm. All you need is a medium size container, like a small trash can. You can buy the red worms through the mail. They come in a squirming mass the size of a softball! These critters consume their own body weight in food each day and convert kitchen scraps into sweet-smelling plant food. The web is loaded with information on using red worms for composting, but here's a site to start with: http://whatcom.wsu.edu/ag/compost/Redwormsedit.htm

Reporter: Can you use compost to grow the same, delicious yellow tomatoes you grow?

LuLu: What a great idea! You'll be amazed at how easy it is.

Squash, snap peas, cucumbers and carrots are also easy to grow. It certainly is a miracle that a tiny tomato seed knows more about making a tomato than all of our human brains put together!

Reporter: Thanks LuLu. Sure hope to come visit you again. Oh, and be sure to sign me up for your CSA!

carrots from my garden

cann

Lulu's greenhouse

Oscar the pig